Kai-lan and the Ladybug Festival

adapted by Mickie Matheis
based on the screenplay "The Ladybug Festival!" written by Sascha Paladino
illustrated by Dave Aikins

Simon Spotlight/Nickelodeon
New York   London   Toronto   Sydney

Ni hao! I'm Kai-lan. I'm going somewhere super special today—the Ladybug Festival!

At the Ladybug Festival there are ladybug games, ladybug rides, and, best of all, the ladybugs do a fan dance in the sky! Do you want to come? Super! C'mon, let's go, go, go!

Here's my grandpa—I call him YeYe. YeYe, *ni hao*! We're going on a hike to the Ladybug Festival.

YeYe ties the lace on my ladybug boot. He always helps me. *Xie xie,* YeYe! Thank you!

"*Bu ke qi,* Kai-lan. You're welcome," says YeYe. "I'll see you at the Ladybug Festival."

YeYe, *yi huir jian.* See you later!

Hooray! Our friends Rintoo the tiger and Hoho the monkey are ready to hike to the Ladybug Festival too. *Ni hao,* Rintoo! *Ni hao,* Hoho!

And here comes our friend Tolee the koala. Wow—his panda backpack is so big! Tolee packed a lot of stuff for the hike: snacks in case we get hungry, binoculars to see birds, a map so we know which way to go, and his stuffed panda, Pandy. *Ni hao,* Tolee! *Ni hao,* Pandy!

Now we're all ready to go. Ladybug Festival, here we come! *Gen wo lai!* Follow me!

Look! There are four paths. Which path goes to the Ladybug Festival? Tolee checks his map and knows which way to go. But before Tolee can say it, Rintoo says we need to go down the gray rock path.

Uh-oh! What did Rintoo find at the end of the gray rock path? Yeah—water! He's all wet. That wasn't the way to the Ladybug Festival.

Tolee is ready to tell us the right way to go. But before he can speak, Hoho says we need to follow the green leaf path.

Uh-oh! Look at Hoho—he's covered with flowers! Hoho is so silly! That path is not the right way to the Ladybug Festival either.

We need to find the right path, or we're going to miss the Ladybug Festival. Do you think Tolee can help us find the way? So do I!

Rintoo and Hoho need to listen to Tolee. But they're being very silly and very loud. They don't know that Tolee has something important to say. They just want to try another path.

Oh, no! Tolee threw his map down and stomped off! He says he's not coming to the Ladybug Festival anymore.

Tolee is our friend. We can't go to the Ladybug Festival without him. Why won't Tolee come with us? Let's find out.

Do you think Tolee won't come with us because Rintoo and Hoho aren't listening to him?

I think so too. Let's ask him.

Tolee, are you not coming to the Ladybug Festival because Hoho and Rintoo aren't listening to you?

"That's right," Tolee says, nodding his head. Tolee looks very sad.

What can we try?
It's up to me and you.
Hoho and Rintoo aren't listening to Tolee.
We'll figure out what to do!

We need to tell Rintoo and Hoho to listen to Tolee.

Rintoo, Hoho, *ting*! Listen! Tolee has something important to say. He knows how to get to the Ladybug Festival.

Rintoo and Hoho turn and listen to Tolee.

"The brown stick path is the one that goes to the Ladybug Festival," Tolee says. "I know because I looked on my map."

Rintoo and Hoho are so happy that they finally listened to Tolee.

"*We got it! We got it! It's really, really true! We got it! We got it! We know just what to do!*" Rintoo and Hoho sing.

When you listen to your friends, you make them feel good. Rintoo and Hoho listened to Tolee, and now we know how to get to the Ladybug Festival.

And Tolee says he'll come with us! Yay! Ladybug Festival, here we come!

We made it to the Ladybug Festival. *Tai hao le!* Super! There's a Ferris wheel, bumper cars, games, and ladybug ice pops. *Hao chi!* Yummy!

And because we listened to Tolee, we made it just in time for the ladybugs' fan dance! Way to go, Tolee!

"*Xie xie,*" says Tolee. "Thanks for listening to me. It made me feel really important."

Bu ke qi, Tolee. You're welcome. You *are* important! You're our friend!

I'm so glad we made it to the Ladybug Festival today. You really helped Rintoo and Hoho listen. And that made Tolee feel good. You are a good friend! And you make my heart feel super happy! *Zai jian!* Good-bye!